In Trouble with Growler Grimes

For Joshua
R.I.

For Daniel
M.W.

Reading Consultant: Prue Goodwin, Lecturer in literacy and children's books

ORCHARD BOOKS
338 Euston Road, London NW1 3BH
Orchard Books Australia
Hachette Children's Books
Level 17/207 Kent Street, Sydney NSW 2000

First published in 2010 by Orchard Books
First paperback publication in 2011

Text © Rose Impey 2010
Illustrations © Melanie Williamson 2010

The rights of Rose Impey to be identified as the author and Melanie Williamson
to be identified as the illustrator of this work have been asserted by them in
accordance with the Copyright, Designs and Patents Act, 1988.

ISBN 978 1 40830 217 0 (hardback)
ISBN 978 1 40830 225 5 (paperback)

1 3 5 7 9 10 8 6 4 2 (hardback)
1 3 5 7 9 10 8 6 4 2 (paperback)
Printed in China

Orchard Books is a division of Hachette Children's Books,
an Hachette UK company.

www.hachette.co.uk

In Trouble with **Growler Grimes**

Written by ROSE IMPEY
Illustrated by MELANIE WILLIAMSON

ORCHARD BOOKS

Nipper McFee was in trouble.
He had overslept again and now he
was late for school.

But more trouble was waiting for him
behind Mr Mewler's corner shop.
Those beastly basement rats were up
to their usual tricks to Get Nipper!

And when Nipper got caught – as he did most days – trouble ran away, laughing.

Then, as usual, trouble followed
Nipper to school, firing water pistols.
At the school gate the teacher,
Mr Growler Grimes, was waiting.

"No weapons allowed in school,"
he growled. "Especially cat-apults!"
"Oh, bother!" Nipper complained.

"What's a cat without a cat-apult?"
he asked.
"Like a banger without a bang,"
said Will.

"No fun at all," agreed Lil.
But even without his catapult, Nipper
managed to get into more trouble.
And when he did, it was right under
the nose of Mr Growler Grimes.

Today those rotten rats had
smuggled in a whoopee cushion.

When Nipper sat down, it made
a very rude noise.

"It wasn't me, Sir," Nipper insisted.
But the teacher saw the evidence
and it had Nipper's name all over it.

It was the third time Nipper had
been in trouble that week.
He was feeling a little
nervous.

Follow me, McFee.

Mr Growler Grimes never used
a cane or a slipper.
The teacher had much worse
punishments up his sleeve.

For the rest of the morning he made Nipper sit with the baby class – wearing an apron.

The rats nearly fell over laughing.

At lunchtime Nipper had to serve
the teachers their lunches, wearing
a waistcoat – and a bow tie!

The rats thought they would burst
with laughter.

And then, after lunch, Mr Growler Grimes made Nipper spend all afternoon with the sewing group.

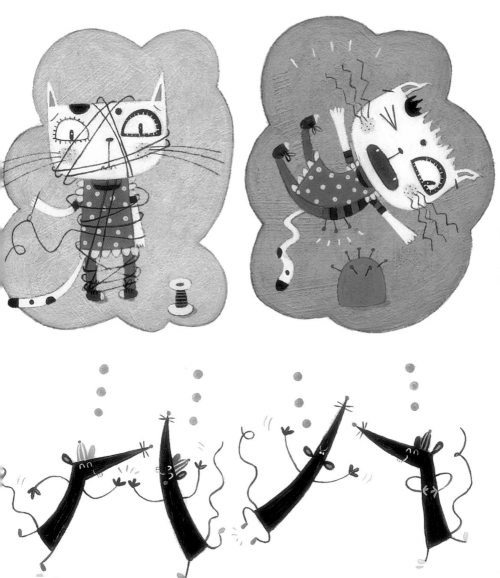

The rats felt as if they had died
and gone to rat heaven.

Will and Lil thought Nipper would
die, too – of shame.
But Nipper didn't look a bit
bothered, because he had a plan.

All afternoon he worked hard on
his plan.
The sewing teacher was very pleased
with Nipper.

She was so pleased she let Nipper
leave school five minutes early.

It gave Nipper extra time . . .

to prepare his revenge.

When the rats came home much later, Nipper and his friends were already waiting for them – up a tree. The rats didn't see them waiting.

They were too busy bragging
about the great trick they'd
played on Nipper.

"Oh boy, did we fix that feline,"
one squealed.
"He never saw it coming,"
squealed another.

And neither did the rats.
Before they knew what was
happening they were well and
truly netted.

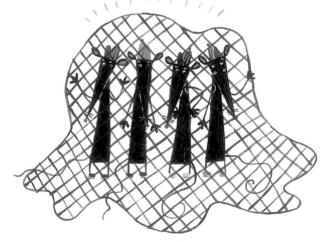

Nipper and his friends slid down
the tree in triumph.
They left the rats tied up, with a
sign that said:

Rubbish. Please take away

Nipper had learned something new: that even a sewing lesson could be useful.

He hoped those rotten rats
had learned a lesson, too. If not,
tomorrow they could write 100 times:
I must not mess with Nipper!

I must not mes
I must not mess with Nipper.
I must not mess with Nipper. I mu
I must not mess with Nipper. I m
I must not mess with Nipper.
I must not m   ith   per. I must
I must not ess   er. I must
I must not ess   Nipper.

ROSE IMPEY ✳ MELANIE WILLIAMSON

All priced at £8.99

Orchard Books are available from all good bookshops,
or can be ordered from our website: www.orchardbooks.co.uk,
or telephone 01235 827702, or fax 01235 827703.

Prices and availability are subject to change.